For Moranne

First edition 2021

Library of Congress Catalog Card Number pending
ISBN 978-1-5362-1562-5

21 22 23 24 25 26 CCP 10 9 8 7 6 5 4 3 2 1

Printed in Shenzhen, Guangdong, China

This book was typeset in Helvetica LT Pro and Iwata GGothic Pro.
The illustrations were created digitally and in watercolor.

Candlewick Press
99 Dover Street
Somerville, Massachusetts 02144

www.candlewick.com

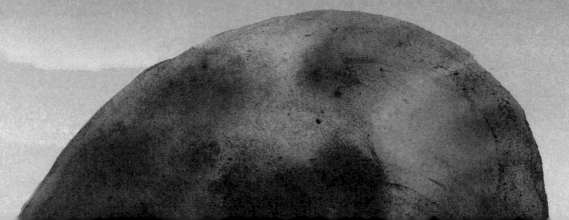

THE

ROCK

FROM

THE

SKY

Jon Klassen

CANDLEWICK PRESS

1.

THE

ROCK

I like standing in this spot. It is my favorite spot to stand.

I don't ever want to stand anywhere else.

Hello.

Hello. What are you doing?

I am standing in my favorite spot. Come. Stand in it with me.

OK.

What do you think
of my spot?

Actually I have a
bad feeling about it.

A bad feeling?

Yes.

There is another spot
over there. Do you see it?

Yes. I see it.

I will go and stand in it,
to see if it feels better
than this spot.

HOW DOES THAT SPOT FEEL?

I CANNOT HEAR YOU.
YOU ARE TOO FAR AWAY.
I AM GOING TO COME BACK.

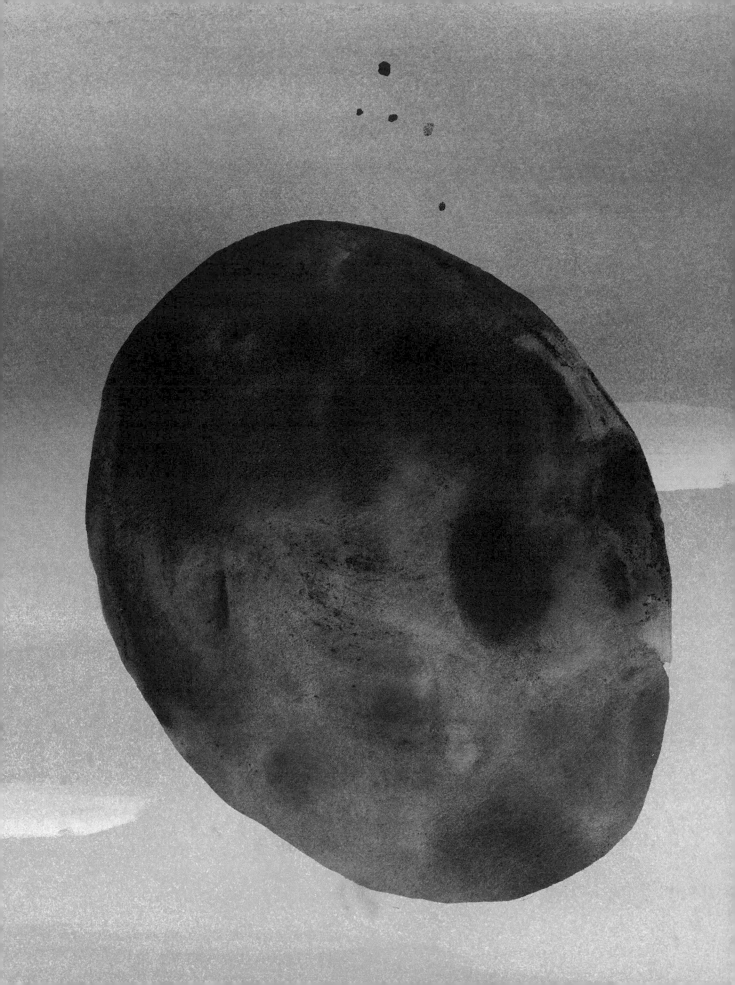

Does this spot still feel bad?

Yes. It feels even worse than before. I am going back to the other spot. Do you want to come with me?

No. I will stay here.
This is my favorite spot.

Are you sure?

Yes.

Oh, hello.
I am standing in
this spot by myself.
Come. Stand in it
with me.

MY SPOT IS BETTER.

YOU ARE TOO FAR AWAY TO HEAR.

I AM COMING CLOSER.

WE STILL CANNOT HEAR YOU.

I said my spot is better.

2.

THE

FALL

Hello.

Hello.

What happened?

Nothing.

Were you
climbing
on it?

No.

Did you
fall off?

No.

Do you need help?

No. I do not need help.

OK.

I never need help.

OK.

What are *you* doing?

I came to take a nap.
It is nice under here.
You can take a nap
too, if you want.
There is just enough
room for two.

No. I am not tired.

OK.

I am never tired.

OK.

3.

THE
FUTURE

What are you doing?

I like to close my eyes and
imagine into the future.

Are you doing it right now?

Yes. Come. Close your eyes
and do it with me.

In the future, this spot will look different.

New things will grow.

New plants and trees will come.

A whole forest maybe.

It is nice here.

Yes. It is.

Wait, what is that?
Does something live here?

Maybe. I don't know.

What is it?

We are in the future.
I don't know what it is.

What is it doing?

SHHH, it will hear you.

AAAAAAAAAAAA!!

OK, OK, I THINK IT'S GOING.

OK, it's gone.

I don't want to imagine into the future with you anymore.

4.

THE

SUNSET

I like to sit and watch
the sunset. My favorite
part is at the very end.

This is a good spot to watch it from. There is nothing in the way.

HELLO.

Hello.

WHAT ARE YOU DOING?

We are watching the sunset.

I DID NOT HEAR YOU. I AM
GOING TO COME CLOSER.

OK. WHAT ARE YOU DOING?

We are watching the sunset.

I STILL CANNOT HEAR YOU.

I AM GOING TO COME CLOSER AGAIN.

OK. What are you doing?

We are not doing it anymore.

5.

NO

MORE

ROOM

I see. I see how it is.
Just enough room for two.

Maybe I will go to the other spot by myself.

Maybe I will never come back.

I SAID MAYBE I WILL NEVER COME BACK.

Maybe I am too far away for them to hear.

I will go back closer and tell them again.

I said maybe I will never come back.